Jimmy Jelly

Rosie and Mum hate Jimmy Jelly's television programme. But they hate him even more when he's there

JACQUELINE WILSON

Jimmy Jelly

Illustrated by Lucy Keijser

BARN OWL BOOKS

To Lauren Elizabeth Carter

First published in Great Britain 1995
by Piccadilly Press Ltd
5 Castle Road, London NW1 8PR
This edition first published 1999
by Barn Owl Books
157 Fortis Green Road, London N10 3LX

Text copyright © Jacqueline Wilson 1995, 1999
Illustrations copyright © Lucy Keijser 1995, 1999
The moral right of Jacqueline Wilson to be identified
as author and Lucy Keijser as illustrator of this work
has been asserted

ISBN 1 903015 01 4

A CIP catalogue record for this book
is available from the British Library

Designed and typeset by Douglas Martin
Printed in China

Chapter One

Do you ever watch Jimmy Jelly on the telly? My little sister Angela is crazy about him.

She doesn't usually watch children's programmes.

She only watches Jimmy Jelly. She

laughs at all his jokes though she doesn't understand them. I'm eight, but I don't always understand them myself actually.

She tries to join in when he sings his silly songs.

She jumps up and down when he

does his daft wobble jelly dance.

She videos every single one of his shows and then she watches him over

and over

and over

again until it's time for his next show.

It drives Mum and me mad.

I can't stick Jimmy Jelly. And neither can Mum. We like to watch *Neighbours* and *Home and Away*.

'Boring' says Angela.

She runs round the room and makes a racket whenever there's anything *we* want to watch.

I get annoyed.

Mum gets annoyed.

Mum gets very cross with Angela.

I can't stick it when Mum gets cross

with me. I get very red in the face.
Sometimes (this is a secret) I even cry.

Angela gets red in the face but she
never cries when Mum tells her off.
Sometimes she laughs, though this
makes Mum get *really mad*. Angela still

doesn't care. My little sister Angela is only four but she can be very *fierce*.

Mum generally wins the battle, but only just. Angela stops running round the room. She sits on the sofa with us. But she doesn't half fidget.

She stops shouting. But she does't keep totally quiet. She *mutters*.

We can't make out exactly what she's saying. Just the odd word or two.

'Mumble mumble mumble Jimmy Jelly,' Angela mutters. 'Jimmy Jelly mumble mumble mumble.'

'Stop mumbling Angela,' says Mum.

Angela glares at her. She stays quiet for a few seconds. Then 'Hiss hiss hiss Jimmy Jelly,' Angela hisses. 'Jimmy Jelly hiss hiss hiss.'

'Angela! says Mum, turning the telly up louder. ' I thought I told you to stop mumbling?'

'I'm not mumbling. I'm *whispering*,' says Angela.

'It's the first sign of madness, mumbling to yourself,' I say.

'I'm not mumbling to myself. I'm talking to Jimmy Jelly,' says Angela.

'What do you mean, you're talking to Jimmy Jelly?' I say. 'He's not on the telly now. It's *Neighbours*.'

'Yes, and we're missing it,' says Mum. 'Sh!'

'I *know* he's not on the telly,' says Angela. 'He's squeezed out of that boxy bit at the back of the telly and he's come to visit me.'

'Oh yes?' I say. 'So where is he then? I can't see him,'

'Of course *you* can't see him,' says Angela. 'I'm the only one that can see him because he's *my* Jimmy Jelly. And budge up a bit on the sofa, Rosie, because you're squashing him.

'You're crazy,' I say.

14

'She's the one that's crazy, isn't she, Jimmy Jelly?' says Angela.

'You're all driving *me* crazy,' says Mum, turning the telly up again. 'I've had a hard day at work and now I just want to relax.'

'Yes, I've had a hard day at school and *I* just want to relax,' I say.

'Yes, I've had a hard day at play and Jimmy Jelly and I want to relax,' says Angela.

Angela plays round at our nan's house on Mondays. She goes to Aunty Pat's on Tuesdays. She goes to Aunty Jean's on Wednesdays. She goes to Mrs Brown up the road on Thursdays. She goes to playschool on Fridays.

They all say they think the world

of our Angela but they can only cope with her one day a week. Now they have to cope with Angela *and* Jimmy Jelly.

Angela and Jimmy Jelly sing silly songs when our nan needs a nap.

Angela and Jimmy Jelly jump up and down in Aunty Pat's small flat.

Angela and Jimmy Jelly tell joke after joke when Aunty Jean has a headache.

Angela and Jimmy Jelly say they don't like Mrs Brown's nice rice pudding and insist they only eat jelly.

Angela and Jimmy Jelly get all the
other children at playschool to tell their
jokes and sing their songs and jump up

18

and down doing their daft wobble jelly
dance.

And Mum and me have to put up

with Angela and Jimmy Jelly
at teatime
and bathtime
and bedtime
and all day Saturday!

Chapter Two

Guess what happens on Sundays!
Angela leaves Jimmy Jelly at home.

We see our dad on Sundays.

Ages ago we were one big family,
Mum and Dad and me and Angela. She
was just a little baby then. Though she
was still fierce.

But then Mum and Dad split up because they had a lot of rows. Angela and I have a lot of rows too, but children don't get divorced.

So now we're two small families. We're Mum and me and Angela on Mondays, Tuesdays, Wednesdays, Thursdays, Fridays and Saturdays.

Dad comes and collects us for the day on Sundays. And then we're Dad and me and Angela.

Mum stays at home. And so does Jimmy Jelly.

Angela kisses Jimmy Jelly goodbye. She kisses him very fondly, lots and lots of times.

Dad did not know what she was doing at first. He doesn't always understand. He especially doesn't understand Angela.

'Angela? What on earth are you doing? Why are you making those weird kissing noises?'

'I'm saying goodbye to Jimmy Jelly,' says Angela.

'Jimmy who? says Dad. He doesn't watch television very much.

'Jimmy Jelly on the telly,' I say.

'I've never heard of him,' says Dad.

'Then you're very lucky,' says Mum. 'We've certainly heard of him, haven't we, Rosie?'

'I'll say,' I say, sighing.

'You go back inside the telly, Jimmy Jelly,' says Angela. 'You stay there till I get home.'

She gives him one last kiss when he's back inside the telly.

'Angela! You're making the screen all smeary,' says Mum.

'Bye bye, Jimmy Jelly,' says Angela, waving at the blank screen. 'Don't be

24

lonely. You can pop out and see mum
for a bit if you really want.'

'Ooh, goodie, goodie!' says Mum.

'But you're not to get *too* friendly.
You're *my* Jimmy Jelly,' says Angela.

'Have you quite done?' says Dad
wearily. 'Can we go now?'

'Yes, Dad,' says Angela, and she takes hold of his hand. 'I'll give you a hello kiss now I've given all my goodbye kisses to Jimmy Jelly.'

We always have a good day out with Dad on Sundays. Sometimes we go to the park.

Sometimes we go to the river.

Sometimes we go all the way to the seaside.

We always eat a lot of lunch.

We have a lot of snacks too.

Angela sometimes feels sick when it's time to go home.

Angela sometimes *is* sick.

She was sick all over me.

'It's a good job Jimmy Jelly stayed at home,' she said. 'He'd have got sicked on too. And he doesn't like sick.'

'I don't like sick either!' I said, mopping me and mopping Angela.

Dad isn't very good when it comes to mopping. But he does give us good days out.

Mum has a good day in.

Sometimes she goes back to bed for an extra snooze.

She reads the Sunday newspapers.

She listens to the radio.

She gardens.

She tries on all her clothes.

She watches the telly.

She doesn't watch Jimmy Jelly. He stays inside. Still and silent.

But he comes rushing out the minute Angela and I get back from our day out with Dad.

Chapter Three

We're going to go to to the Shopping Centre on Saturday,' says Mum.

'Oh good,' I say. I like shopping.

'Oh bad,' Angela says. She hates shopping.

'No, Angela, you're going to want to come this special Saturday,' says Mum, waving the local paper at us.

She shows us this big photo on the front.

'Who's this, Angela?' says Mum.

Angela stares.

'It's Jimmy Jelly!' she says.

'That's right! Jimmy Jelly is coming to our Shopping Centre this Saturday. He's opening up this big new music shop,' says Mum.

Angela looks very surprised. 'He didn't say anything about it to me,' she says.

'No darling, this is the *real* Jimmy Jelly. You'll be able to see him on Saturday,' says Mum.

'I can see him any day I want,' says

Angela. She puts her arms up and hugs
thin air. 'Can't I, Jimmy Jelly?'

Mum shakes her head and sighs
to me.

'Maybe she's too little to understand,
Rosie,' she says. 'Never mind. Just wait
till Saturday. She'll be so excited.'

32

Angela doesn't *act* excited on Saturday. She makes a fuss when Mum tries to hurry her up.

'Switch the video off, Angela, and run and get your clothes on,' says Mum.

'But I want to watch Jimmy Jelly!'

'We're going to see the real Jimmy Jelly, Angela, I keep telling you. That's why we want to go to the Shopping Centre early. So we can get a good place at the front of the crowd,' says Mum.

There are crowds and crowds and crowds down at the Shopping Centre. Mum holds our hands tightly in case we get lost. Angela wriggles and fusses and tries to pull her hand away.

'No, Mum. I'm holding Jimmy Jelly's hand,' says Angela.

At the sound of Jimmy Jelly's name all the heads turn and stare at my little sister. They think she's maybe *really* holding Jimmy Jelly's hand. Mum and I grin and wriggle.

Angela glares.

'I don't like all these people,' she moans. 'I'm getting squashed.'

'Here, darling, you squeeze in front of me,' says a kind lady.

There are lots of kind ladies. It's not long before Angela is right at the front. And Mum and me.

'Aren't we lucky, girls?' says Mum.

'Why?' says Angela. 'This is boring

just standing and I'm still getting squashed.'

'Stop moaning, Angela,' I say. 'Jimmy Jelly's going to be here in a minute.'

'There he is!' Mum says, pointing.

'Jimmy Jelly!' everyone shouts.

Jimmy Jelly jumps up on to the platform and waves and smiles at everyone.

'Wave, Angela,' says Mum. 'It's Jimmy Jelly!'

Mum waves. I wave. All the crowd waves. All the crowd except Angela.

'Hi everyone,' says Jimmy Jelly. 'It feels strange stuck up here all on my ownsome. Who wants to come and keep me company, eh?'

He peers all round the crowd. Mum pushes Angela forward.

'Here's your number one fan, Jimmy Jelly,' says Mum, and she lifts Angela on to the platform.

'Hi there poppet. What's your name, eh?' says Jimmy Jelly.

Angela lowers her head and presses
her lips together. She doesn't say a
word.

'Angela! Tell Jimmy Jelly your name,'
I hiss.

Jimmy Jelly looks at me. And Mum.

'Come on, girls,' he says, helping us on to the platform too.

We tell Jimmy Jelly our names. We laugh when Jimmy Jelly tells a joke.

We join in when he sings his silly song.

We jump up and down when he does his daft wobble jelly dance.

We know exactly what to do because we've watched him over and over again.

Angela knows what to do too. But she doesn't do it. She just stands there.

She won't laugh, she won't sing, she won't dance.

'I'm ever so sorry, Jimmy Jelly,' says Mum. 'I don't know what's up with her.'

'Never mind, I expect she's just a bit shy,' says Jimmy Jelly, and he picks Angela up and gives her a kiss.

Angela goes very pink, but she still doesn't say a word.

Jimmy Jelly gives me a kiss too. And Mum.

And he gives us a signed Jimmy Jelly poster and a Jimmy Jelly badge and a Jimmy Jelly balloon.

Everyone stares at us as we climb down from the platform. It's as if we're almost as famous as Jimmy Jelly.

'Oh goodness, weren't we lucky?' says Mum.

'He's much nicer than I thought, old Jimmy Jelly,' I say.

But Angela still says nothing at all.

'Whatever's the matter with you, Angela?' says Mum. 'You're not usually shy.'

'I'm *not* shy,' says Angela.

'So why on earth didn't you talk to Jimmy Jelly?' I say.

'That wasn't Jimmy Jelly!' says Angela.

'Of course it was, Angela,' says Mum.

'That wasn't *my* Jimmy Jelly,' said Angela. 'I didn't like *that* Jimmy Jelly one bit.'

She doesn't even want to wear the Jimmy Jelly badge or carry the Jimmy Jelly balloon.

So I have them instead.

I want the poster too, to pin over my bed.

'No, I want the poster,' says Mum.
'You've got the badge and balloon,
Rosie.'

We argue about it all the way home.

'Those two are driving me crazy,' says Angela to *her* Jimmy Jelly.

Then we all squash up on the sofa and watch Jimmy Jelly on telly.

All About Barn Owl Books

If you've ever scoured the bookshops for that book you loved as a child
or the one your children wanted to hear again and again and been
frustrated then you'll know why Barn Owl Books exists. We are hoping
to bring back many of the excellent books that have slipped from
publishers' backlists in the last few years.

Barn Owl is devoted entirely to reprinting worthwhile out-of-print
children's books. Initially we will not be doing any picture books, purely
because of the high costs involved, but any other kind of children's book
will be considered. We are always on the lookout for new titles and hope
that the public will help by letting us know what their own special
favourites are. If anyone would like to photocopy and fill in the form
below and give us their suggestions for future titles we would be delighted.

We do hope that you enjoyed this book and will read our other
Barn Owl titles.

Books I would like to see back in print include:

_____
_____
_____
_____

Signature
_____

Address
_____
_____

Please return to Ann Jungman, Barn Owl Books
15 New Cavendish Street, London WIM 7AL

Barn Owl Books

THE PUBLISHING HOUSE DEVOTED ENTIRELY TO
THE REPRINTING OF CHILDREN S BOOKS

TITLES AUTUMN 1999

Jimmy Jelly — Jacqueline Wilson

Angela just loves Jimmy Jelly when she sees him on tv. It's a bit different when she meets him in the flesh. A charming story for first readers. (£3.99)

Private — Keep Out! — Gwen Grant

The hilarious story of a family growing up immediately after the war. Told by the anarchic and rebellious diary-keeping youngest sister . . . it is ideal for confident readers. (£4.99)

You're thinking about doughnuts — Michael Rosen

When Frank is left alone in the museum, while his mother does the cleaning, he doesn't expect the skeleton to come alive and introduce him to the exhibits. A gripping read for the confident reader. (£4.99)

Voyage — Adèle Geras

The story of a group of migrants leaving Russia for the USA in 1905. During the weeks at sea, hopes and fears surface and love is explored as they wait for the great adventure in the New World to begin. Suitable for teenagers. (£4.99)

TITLES PLANNED FOR 2000

The Mustang Machine — Chris Powling

Your guess is as good as mine — Bernard Ashley

Hairs in the palm of the hand — Jan Mark

The Little Dragon Steps Out — Ann Jungman